A Night in the Bishop House

Ronda L. Caudill, PhD

A Night at the Bishop House. Copyright © 2012

by Ronda L. Caudill, Ph.D.

ISBN: 978-0615846477

ISBN: 0615846475

Edited by Melissa Day

Cover Photography purchased from IStock Photo

First edition September 2012

DEDICATION

This book is dedicated to my wonderful husband Ricky, my awesome daughters Brittany and Nikita, and to my amazing son-in-law Travis. Thank you all for the love, encouragement, and inspiration.

It was warm and sticky that stormy June night and the wind blew wildly. The thunder boomed with great explosions while lightning flooded the night sky. The tattered shutters beat against the old whitewashed house with loud crashes hanging on dearly as the wind ripped at them. The old wooden siding danced in the wind where it had long ago released its grasp on the house. The weeds and underbrush that sprawled out against the house waved violently in the wind.

With the pouring rain beating down upon my head, I had no other choice but to enter the old abandoned house on the outskirts of town. As I approached the front porch, I felt an eerie sensation of being watched from the windows. An especially menacing feeling came from the attic and the cellar. The house had not been occupied since its original owners, the Bishops, lived there in the early 1800s. This grand old home had been built to house a large family—a family with many laughing children. This, however, was not its destiny.

I never travel the route by that house, for the house terrifies me. But on that particular night I was forced to go that way. The storm came from nowhere. That morning while I was listening to the news and sipping my coffee—which consisted more of cream and sugar than coffee—the weatherman called for clear skies. And clear skies were what we had that night when I left the dinner party that I had reluctantly attended.

The party was a birthday party for my boss. I had been dreading it for over a month, ever since the afternoon I had found the invitation with my name on it, Victoria May Long, lying on my desk. I'm not an antisocial person; it's just that I don't have friends at work. I go, sit at my desk and do my job—no distractions. So, I went to this party out of courtesy. I stayed as long as I could, pretending not to hate every minute there. Finally, I had stayed long enough to politely excuse myself and go home. I think I was the first to leave, but maybe no one would notice I had left early.

My boss only lived ten miles from my home. About three miles away from my house the road forked. One route went by the river and a small subdivision of houses built back in the 1950s when a small company had come to Summerland, West Virginia and set up. The company created a few jobs in this small community. However, about twenty years later the company folded and the jobs disappeared. This small subdivision built for corporate employees served as a reminder of the company's hay day.

The second route went by the Bishop house and a long stretch of deserted woods. Mist loomed over the trees. The scene was complete with the echoing sounds of wolves howling and owls screeching. I avoided that route at all costs, never going that way unless it was absolutely necessary. That route was desolate and spooky. I had only been that way a few times. As an adult, I had traveled that way a couple of times with friends to save time. And I had never taken that route after dark—until tonight.

As I left the party that night, the weather was clear. However, it began to rain not far from my boss's house. The further I drove, the worse the weather became, until eventually the storm had transformed into a raging beast. About a half mile before the fork, I had to swerve to miss a large, fallen, maple tree. I was forced to detour by the Bishop house because the old maple tree was blocking the river route. So, to my dismay, I was forced to take the route by the deserted stretch of woods and the Bishop house.

When I saw that fallen tree blocking the road, the harsh realization hit me that I would have to travel by that house, the house that I had avoided for many, many years. My heart sank and I felt sick to my stomach. The last time I felt this sick was when I'd downed an entire bottle of Jack Daniels after a bad interview. In addition to my upset stomach, my knees went weak like I had just run a marathon. I became lightheaded as though I had been scuba diving and resurfaced too quickly. In spite of everything I was feeling, I had no choice but to drive forward.

As my car moved swiftly forward through the darkness, I tried hard to think of other things. I thought about work, friends, family and even that dinner party I just left. Less than an hour ago

I couldn't wait to leave. Now I longed to be back there with my boss, my colleagues, bad food, cheap wine and terrible conversation. That situation seemed wonderful compared to my current one.

The three-mile stretch of spooky woods around the Bishop house was obviously not traveled often. While the other route was kept clean and pristine with no potholes, no ragged shoulders, and well-kept yards, this road was unkempt, with potholes, ragged shoulders, and no lane markers painted. The grass had not been mowed, and tree limbs hung out over the road like a teasing trapeze artist. There were no other houses besides the Bishop house.

Though it was less than three miles to my home from there, it felt like three hundred lay before me. It was rainy, dark and terribly frightening. The Bishop house was only about a mile past the fork. As I approached, I became more apprehensive. I resolved to keep her eyes straight ahead on the road. I would not look in the direction of the house. I was terrified of what I might see.

As I approached the house, I could barely see two feet in front of me. The rain beat so hard on the windshield that, even with the wipers on high, I still had problems seeing the road. I was focused so hard on driving through the miserable storm that I hardly noticed the Bishop house right next to me.

Then it happened. My car died. I was devastated at my

luck—or lack thereof. I couldn't believe that of all the places for my car to die it had to be there. I sat there for about forty-five minutes, the first ten or fifteen of which were spent trying to revive my piece-of-shit car. If I made it out of this unscathed, first thing the next morning I was going to the dealership to raise hell.

I waited on the storm to ease up, but it did not. I had no cell phone reception because of the storm so I couldn't call for help. I had no idea what I should do. I thought about walking—after all, it was only two more miles. I could do that easily. But not in this storm. Not tonight.

The longer I waited, the more violent the storm became. The old, weak, tree limbs hung out over the road ready to plummet to the ground at any moment. Small branches kept falling all around me. My little car wasn't much protection from a large limb or a tree. I dawdled as long as could trying to make a decision. Finally, I bolted toward the house, through the yard and onto the porch. Reluctantly, I reached for the doorknob, but before my hand touched the doorknob the door opened by an unseen hand. I stepped through the entryway unsure of what I would find.

I knew I either had to stay in the horrid house with whatever evil lurked around the next corner, or go out to face the monstrous storm. Reluctantly, I decided to stay in the house of horror, at least until the beast outside had subsided. As I stepped inside, I felt like I could see, hear and smell death. Fear took over my very soul. I felt as if something or someone evil was with me. Staring at me. Following me.

The door behind me closed and I whirled around to see who had pushed it. I found nothing but darkness and periodic flashes of lightning shining through the tattered and torn curtains on the window. I tried to decide what to do next. Should I stand there in the foyer with my back to the door all night scared as hell, or should I try to find an old oil lamp to give me more light than the sporadic lightning flashes? Maybe some mischievous kids had come into the house on a dare or something. Maybe they had fled hurriedly and left behind a flashlight or lantern.

There was a third option. I could run out of that house and never look back. I could keep running, not stopping for anyone or anything, until I reached the safety of my own home. Alas, this didn't seem to be very realistic, due to the terrible storm raging outside.

So, I pulled together all the courage I could find within myself and searched for a light source. It was bad enough that I had to be alone, but the dark was too unbearable to fathom. This option was going to be difficult, I knew. I could only see, and even then not very well, when lightning flashed through the old windows.

I waited on the lightning and looked around quickly, trying to decide which direction to go. Each time lightning danced through the threads of curtains, I tried to locate anything I could use to get a sense of the place. The first flash gave me a glimpse of the room to my left and of the hallway ahead of me. The next flash gave enough light to see the room to my right. I was also able to make out the grand staircase and, to my luck, an old oil lamp on a small antique table just a few feet to my right. I don't know how I had missed it before.

The antique table was beautifully carved out of dark wood. I had once heard that all the furnishings in the house were original. The house had been left just the way it was the day they took Sarah Bishop away.

Now that I had an oil lamp, I needed to light it. I was in luck again. I still had a lighter in my purse from a camping trip I had taken with friends the previous weekend. I pulled the lighter from my purse and lit the lamp, which still had a small bit of oil in it. And like magic, I had light. Electricity had never been installed in the old home because the Bishops were the only ones to reside in it, so this oil lamp was my only source of light.

There had been talk of converting the house into a bed and breakfast or a historic museum, since no one had ever claimed the house and it reverted back to the town's possession. However, when anyone would mention something of this nature, strange things would happen around the old place and the plans would always fall through.

When the light illuminated the house, I was awestricken beholding the splendor and beauty of the magnificent place. But I knew in my heart that its beauty was deceiving.

It was a grand, stately home with four levels—two stories, an attic and a cellar. The kitchen was detached from the rest of the house to prevent fires and overheating during the summer months, which was a normal design for the period in which this house was built. Many homes built in that time period would eventually succumb to renovations and modernization. The Bishop house, though, had not changed at all; it only showed age.

I decided to satisfy an odd sense of morbid curiosity, even though I had never had any desire to go into the house before that night. I suppose I avoided that house because it reminded me of nightmares I had as a child. However, now that I was in the house something compelled me to explore it.

I told myself I needed to find a blanket and something to burn in order to get warm and dry. I was cold from being drenched in the rain. Even though the air outside was still quite warm, the air inside the house was cold, damp, and musty.

The air in the house reminded me of my grandmother's cellar where I hid once as a child. I thought I saw something in there. It was indescribable, but felt evil, and I fled the cellar never to enter it again. Even as an adult I would not step foot in that cellar.

I felt a compelling urgency to ascend the grand staircase and explore the second floor, even though I was filled with anxiety. Once I topped the stairs, I had the odd sensation of familiarity. The staircase sprawled out on both sides like a flower in full bloom leading to two wings at the top. One hallway led to the left and one led to the right.

I had a bad feeling about continuing, but something inside forced me onward. I went down the hallway to my right. There were so many rooms. The hallway was peppered with doors. The old wallpaper lining the hallway was torn and tattered. The once beautifully stained wainscoting was now weathered and chipped, with holes here and there where mice had made their homes. Parts of the trim around the faded wood had long ago fallen off the wall.

All the doors down the hallway were closed. As I approached the first door, I felt very apprehensive. I reached down and twisted the cold, marble doorknob, then pushed the door open slowly as the hinges creaked eerily. Curiosity overpowered my terror and I peeped around the door. To my amazement nothing jumped out and grabbed me.

I mustered a bit more courage and cautiously walked into the antique-filled room. I'm sure it once was a beautiful room in its day. But now the wallpaper hung by threads and the ceiling crumbled in spots. Oil lamps were on the tables, moth-eaten linens lined the bed and tattered curtains clung to the windows.

I felt as if someone was watching my every move, but each time I turned to catch a glimpse of someone behind me in the dark no one was there. The unseen presence was unnerving. When I could stand no, more I walked out. I turned back to leave the door as I found it but, for some reason, changed my mind and left it open.

I went on to the next door. This room was very similar, but the wallpaper was different. I had the same uneasy feeling of being watched. I left this door open as well. The next room was the same, and the next, and the next. I went to the end of the hallway, making my way through every room, alternating from one side to the other leaving every door open. After I had explored the last room I turned to walk back down the hallway in the direction from which I had come, and all the doors I had left open were now closed. I turned to the door of the room I had just explored, and it suddenly slammed shut. I ran down the hallway.

At the end of the hallway I stopped to catch my breath and gather more ever-fading courage. Finally, after what must have been twenty minutes, I regained enough courage to get my legs to move down the next hallway. It, too, was peppered with doors, and they were all closed. I began to explore and, as I expected, all the rooms were similar—that is, until I reached the last room.

It was much larger and had a beautiful entryway. As I stepped inside, I stumbled down three wide steps. I had just wandered into what must have been the master bedroom.

It was a stately room with a grand fireplace and a beautiful crystal chandelier. The chandelier was draped in black—handcrafted and sculpted black iron, undoubtedly painstakingly pitched by the local blacksmith of the day. And how beautiful it still was. Crystal teardrops hung from every inch of it. The teardrops caught the reflection of my oil lamp and showed every color in the spectrum. The crystals were so beautifully cut; they sparkled like diamonds.

The room was filled with antique furniture, just as in the other rooms, including a bed fit for royalty with a canopy clinging to the falling plaster above the headboard. To match the bed was a beautiful hand-carved dresser, an armoire, and a vanity with a mirror so old it had black etchings, preventing a full reflection.

Lying on the vanity was a silver brush and mirror set. There was something disturbing about the set. Thick dust covered everything from decades of neglect. Yet the silver set rested upon the dust beside a dust-free spot in the shape of the brush and mirror. It had apparently been moved recently.

I raised my head to explore the rest of the room and my eyes caught two images in the old mirror. One image was my own, and the other appeared to be a woman. I couldn't tell much about the reflection. Maybe this was the person who had been watching me since I came into the house. When I turned to ask her if she lived there, to apologize for intruding and to explain why I was in her home, she was no longer there. Maybe it was my imagination. Maybe no one had been there at all. I needed to get back downstairs to the living room, start a fire and control my senses.

Across the room, holding dearly to the crumbling bricks above the fireplace, was a portrait of a beautiful young woman. She was dressed in black, with hair of ebony spirals and blue eyes that looked as though they had been sculpted from the same crystal as the chandelier in the center of the room.

Still, there was something amiss. The crystalline eyes of the ebony haired woman from the painting looked cold and empty. I felt as if her stare had a hold over me, keeping me still, entrancing me. For some unknown reason I knew the portrait was of Sarah Bishop.

After a long examination of the portrait, I turned to leave. I had had enough of this room, the creepy reflection, the silver brush set and the captivating portrait. But I took another quick glance at the bed and saw a hand-quilted blanket that had been eaten through from rot, decay and moths. It was probably beautiful in its day, but now only threads. Perhaps it would still help me recover from the cold. So, I picked it up and made my way hastily out of the room, feeling once again as if I were being watched.

Was it the woman whose reflection I had just seen alongside my own in that old mirror? Was she still there but not wishing to show herself? Was this woman Sarah Bishop?

I had to get out of that room. I walked through the doorway and turned to grasp the cold marble doorknob, but before I could, the door slammed hard in my face. I was terrified.

When I turned to walk back down the hallway, something was different. Actually, it was just as I had left it, which was the odd thing. All the doors were still open, unlike the first hallway. I took a step down the hallway, and nothing happened. I took another step, then another and another, and still nothing happened. Then when I reached the first door along my gauntlet, it slammed to the right of me. Apprehensively I made my way to the next room, and that door slammed to the left of me. And so it went all the way back down the hallway until I reached the last door. Now all the doors were once again closed. And yet, I wasn't at all surprised—frightened, but not surprised.

I went back to the living room, tired from exploration and exhausted from fear. I hadn't noticed this room in much detail earlier. Now that I was actually in the room, I looked closely at every detail, scrutinizing everything in the room. The living room was bombarded with antique furniture, including a feather-filled couch with long black fringe and an intricately carved rich mahogany frame. I also noticed a crystal chandelier, much like the one from the upstairs bedroom. There was also a beautiful fireplace. This fireplace, however, was much larger than the one from the bedroom; it was about six feet high and about ten feet wide. The woodwork on the mantle had the same intricate detail as the woodwork in the rest of the room—the rest of the house. The wooden trim throughout the house looked as though it had been painstakingly hand- carved, and with excruciating care.

Above this fireplace hung another portrait. It was of the same woman with the crystalline blue eyes from the portrait upstairs. In this painting, she was accompanied by a gentle looking man with warm, brown eyes and a caring, sad look about him. Unbeknownst to me I knew this to be John Bishop. He had dark, collar-length hair, a medium build and a fair complexion. I felt as though he was staring at me.

The painting was so realistic that, even upon close examination, I could see no brush strokes. At one point, I could have sworn the eyes blinked. Also, at times it looked as though the characters were breathing, their chests moving ever so slightly in and out. I must have been hallucinating. Maybe there was some type of scentless toxin in the air affecting my head.

I tossed the old blanket I had been clinging to onto the black couch. I noticed beside the fireplace on the floor was a large brass basket with scraps of wood for kindling, as well as a couple of small logs. I knew the wood would not burn long, but I needed some type of warmth, if only for a short while. I built a fire.

While waiting on the fire to warm the room a little, I heard a loud crash from another room. I was sure there was someone or something else in the house with me and I couldn't just sit there and wait on whomever or whatever it was to get the jump on me. Reluctantly, I went to find the source of the crash. After all, I was here for the rest of the night, and I was not in the mood to kick back in front of the fire, pull out a good book to read and relax.

The ground level wrapped around in a huge circle. From the living room I moved to the adjoining room. I suppose it was probably a parlor of some kind. It was as beautiful as the living room, filled with expensive antique furniture, area rugs, oil lamps, paintings, a smaller crystal chandelier and a smaller fireplace. And I had the same eerie feeling of being watched.

Then I heard something on the other side of the room. It sounded like light footsteps creaking on loose floorboards. I spun around, but found no one. All I saw was the rain beading down the windowpane. As I gazed upon the window, the beads began to look like streams of tears.

I went into the next room. The room appeared to be another parlor or sitting room, with a fireplace and chandelier, filled with beautiful antique furniture, no different from any other room in the house. Again, I felt as if I were being watched.

The next room, however, was much different than the others. It was larger, for one thing. The center of the room was empty, although couches, love seats and chairs lined the walls. Small tables surrounded the seats. While the other floors had been hard wood, this floor was constructed of beautiful black marble. At one end of the room was a stage. Chairs were lined up in three semicircular rows, with old music stands in front of them. It looked as if it had been set up for a small orchestra to play. At the center of the stage was a grand piano, just waiting for a young prodigy to sit down and lovingly stroke its keys.

The room had three large chandeliers with the same crystal angel tears hanging from them, and two huge fireplaces with crumbling bricks barely clinging to one another. The room had pocket doors that slid into the walls.

I stood in the middle of the room and closed my eyes as something took over me. I could almost hear the sound of the orchestra playing beautiful music and many people laughing and talking. The sounds were so realistic; I could imagine beautiful women in ball gowns latched onto the arms of handsome men in old-fashioned suits. Some were mingling and talking, others were dancing, whirling around like music box figurines. It was then that I realized, of course, I was in the ballroom.

The house felt oddly familiar. I was still frightened, but I was also so morbidly curious and so filled with amazement, awestricken by the sheer beauty of the place, that the fear was temporarily pushed aside.

I had a compelling urge to walk around this room—on the ballroom floor. For some unexplained reason I found myself dancing—whirling around on the ballroom floor. With my eyes still closed, I felt like a child, pretending to be one of the ballroom belles dancing with handsome, young, southern gentlemen. The floor was so smooth under my feet, I felt like I was floating. The room echoed with every step I took. I felt as though I had stepped back in time.

Then I opened my eyes. The room was filled with people, dressed for a masquerade ball. The women wore fancy dresses, complete with ribbons, ruffles and bows, just like I had imagined, and the men wore distinguished three-piece suits. Some wore masks and some did not. The faces I could see were all so beautiful.

These were the most beautiful people I had ever seen. Never before had I imagined there could be such beauty. They were all so sensual, their movements smooth and effortless.

The room also looked different. It was clean and the wallpaper was intact, no crumbling bricks, and no rat holes in the walls. I knew I must have been hallucinating, but it seemed so real. I spotted a reflection in one of the windows and realized it was my own.

Everything about me was different. I wore a beautiful ball gown, just like the other women. My hair was pulled back and put up with long black ringlets. In my hand, I held a beautiful feathered mask similar to the ones the other women were holding. I knew then I must have been having a breakdown. I had totally lost my mind. I closed my eyes and shook my head, trying to regain my sanity and come back to reality.

Then I felt someone tap me on the shoulder. I turned to find a man standing there. He asked me to dance with him. When he lowered his mask, I recognized him as the man from the painting, the man I knew was John Bishop. We began to waltz. I had never learned to waltz, so I was surprised when we started dancing that I knew how. The man's hands were soft and warm, and he had a gentle touch. His eyes were kind. If it's true that the eyes are windows to the soul, then he must have been an angel. I found myself comfortably lost in his eyes. I could not look away from him. Everything about him was perfect—his lips, his nose and his soft, dark hair. He seemed like perfection from God's own hands.

If this was John Bishop, and I was not hallucinating but somehow experiencing his being, I wondered how he ended up with the cold woman from the portrait. We danced without a word for what seemed like hours.

Then, at the end of the last dance, he dipped me backward and leaned in to kiss me ever so gently. His kiss caused a fire to rage inside me. I felt my entire body flush. I felt like I had just fallen in love. But that was ridiculous. This man was either a crazy hallucination or a ghost— either way, nothing good could come of it, least of all a love affair.

He lifted me up, still holding me in his arms. At that moment, I felt another tap on my shoulder. But this time when I turned around, I was not so pleasantly surprised. It was the woman from the painting—it was Sarah Bishop. Her crystalline eyes were piercing, and her face was drawn tight with anger. Her words thundered, as she demanded to know why I was kissing her husband.

I turned to say something to him, but my words came out stammered and senseless. And then he was gone, just like that. I turned back to face the woman alone, but she was leaving the room, floating away from me. She floated through the rooms, one by one.

Terrified but entranced, I had to follow her. I followed as she entered the library, a room I had not yet explored. It was marvelous. Bookshelves lined all four walls from floor to ceiling. Large rolling ladders made of sculpted iron were on every wall. The shelves overflowed with beautiful leather-bound books of every color imaginable.

A desk sat in the middle of the room, along with a matching chair. They were made of the same beautiful dark wood with magnificent carving. This room was fit for royalty. I had never seen anything to match its splendor.

The woman pulled a book from one of the shelves, revealing a secret entrance. Stupidly, I followed her in. The entrance led up a set of spiral iron stairs to the attic. I was not prepared for what I saw next.

The room was filled with paraphernalia of evil. A wooden pedestal in the middle of the room had an open book upon it. I dared not lay my eyes upon its pages for fear of what I might behold. I looked around more. I saw jars of herbs, jars filled with animal body parts, more books, a crooked wooden wand and an altar with crystals and a knife upon it. Then I realized the woman had disappeared. There must have been another passage that led out to a different room.

Suddenly, the woman appeared to me just as quickly as she had disappeared. She glared at me with her cold eyes, as if it were last few minutes of my life. The door slammed shut behind me. I ran over to it and frantically tried to force it open, but to no avail. I was trapped in a hidden room, in a haunted house that no one ever enters, with a furious specter.

Then I felt a soft touch on my shoulder. When I turned, the man from the painting and the ballroom stood in front of me. At that moment, the doorknob clicked and turned, and the door opened. I ran back down the stairs toward the library, ready to leave the house. I hadn't gotten very far when I lost my footing and fell down the steps.

I bumped my head and lost consciousness. I'm not sure how long I lay there on the floor. But when I awoke, I had a massive headache and my vision was blurry. I felt like I had gone nine rounds with a heavyweight champion. I slowly and painfully made my way back to the living room. On my way back, I saw no sign of the woman, the man, or the strange guests I had seen in the ballroom. I found another oil lamp and lit it with my lighter. Then I made my way to the couch.

I reluctantly lay down on the black feather-filled couch. I pulled the quilt of few threads over me that was lying on the couch and curled into the fetal position, fright and insecurity weighing uneasily in the pit of my stomach. My mind raced with stories of the Bishop house.

I began to remember the folklore about the house and its owners. I felt lightheaded, as though I might black out again. My head throbbed. As I thought about the stories surrounding the house, the line between memory and hallucination blurred and I slowly drifted back into unconsciousness.

The story goes that, many years ago, a young wealthy aristocrat named John Bishop had fallen in love with and, after a short courtship, married a beautiful young woman named Sarah, who was said to have descended from witches of Salem Village. John was a gentleman of logic and reason, and did not take stock in tales of witches and devils. He never thought anything of the rumors about his beautiful bride because he loved her dearly. Little did he know he was under her spell.

John built Sarah the house of her dreams in 1823, the Bishop house. It was a glorious home in all its splendor. Sarah had overseen every little detail in its creation. Since John was so wealthy, money was of no object to him. He only wanted his lovely young bride to be happy. It was said that he had once uttered aloud that he would gladly sell his soul if it would please his wife.

John gave Sarah everything she wanted, except a child. He tried everything he could think of to please her, to make up for their childlessness. He doted over her, showered her with lavish gifts, and answered to her every whim. But nothing could make up for the absence of a child, and she grew to hate her husband for his barrenness. Sarah took advantage of John and the guilt he felt. The older Sarah grew, the more spiteful she became.

The rumors about Sarah increased along with her hatred toward her husband. The townspeople began to talk. They claimed Sarah was carrying on her family tradition of witchcraft, that she was in league with the devil himself and that the hounds of hell guarded her from harm. Nevertheless, John would not believe that his Sarah was a witch. Even though she had beaten him down and treated him like an unwanted animal, he still loved her. Some say he even uttered the words, "I love you," as she took her revenge on him the day she snapped.

That fateful day, Sarah ranted and raved about having no family because of John. John was apologetic. But Sarah could take no more. She ran to the shed, with John following and groveling close behind, and grabbed hold of an axe. She swung it around and, without taking aim, cut John's head completely off. The poor man never knew what hit him. Sarah then snatched up a torch stake and drove it into the ground with the handle of the axe. She grabbed John's head and with one fluid motion, thrust it down upon the torch stake. To this day, no one has ever found John Bishop's body. Some say the devil took it away. Others think the hounds of hell devoured it. No one knows for certain what became of John's body.

The servants were so frightened; they fled into town to get help. When the townspeople arrived, they were horrified to see what the witch had done to poor John. They found Sarah in the house, covered in blood, sitting on the living room floor, laughing.

They yanked her up and dragged her, kicking and screaming, out of the house. They tied her to a horse and dragged her into town. With her clothes torn half off and her body battered and bruised, they hoisted her up onto the gallows, where she was promptly hanged in front of all the townspeople. Sarah was never given a trial or a chance to defend herself; it was old-fashioned justice.

After her limbs stopped twitching and all the life was gone from her limp body, they cut her down and displayed her corpse in front of the jail for all to bear witness upon. There was only one problem, the next day, Sarah's body was nowhere to be found. Some speculated that she was raised from the dead by the hand of Satan, while others contest that a bunch of mischievous children stole her corpse and hid it as a joke. Whatever happened, no one would ever know. The corpse of Sarah Bishop was never found.

I woke up with a start. I found myself sitting straight up on the black, feather-filled couch. I then remembered that this was not the end of the Sarah Bishop story.

Every man who had a hand in the hanging of Sarah Bishop mysteriously died or disappeared. One man was ripped to shreds by a pack of wild dogs. Another, who was an excellent swimmer, drowned. And still another simply disappeared from his bed one night. The list goes on.

There was much speculation surrounding Sarah Bishop's action's. To this day, some believe Sarah wanted to be killed and, with the help of Satan, was reincarnated as something else. Others believe she still resides in the house as an evil spirit.

I began to wonder if Sarah Bishop still roamed around the old house. I pondered all the stories I had heard about Sarah and the house throughout the years. Were the things I had experienced real, or were they all just hallucinations? Fear swept over me like a tidal wave. As cold as the house was, I began to sweat. I heard noises coming from the cellar that sounded like an argument between a man and a woman. The voices belonged to the man with whom I had danced and the woman I had followed into the attic. I froze with fear. After a few minutes, I managed to get up and slowly move toward the cellar door, the old oil lamp in one hand to light the way down the long dank hallway. The closer I got to the door, the louder the voices became.

I finally reached the door and, with trembling hands, reached down to grab the doorknob. But before I could, the door swung open, making me stagger backwards. Out came the woman from the paintings. Following closely behind was the man, the man from the painting in the living room, the man I had danced with in the ballroom, the man who had unlocked the attic door to help me escape. Sarah and John Bishop. They ran past me, as if I weren't there. They took absolutely no notice of me.

For reasons I cannot explain, I followed them. I had the same sense of curiosity when I had followed the woman into the attic. The couple ran out into the yard, off of the porch, and out to the shed. As I realized what was unfolding in front of me, I knew exactly what was to come next. I ran into the rain-soaked yard. I watched helplessly as Sarah grabbed the axe and thrust the blade into John's neck. His body fell limp to the ground as his head rolled in the other direction. Then fear took hold of me.

Sarah looked at me and gave John's head a swift kick in my direction. She laughed as John's head rolled to my feet.

Her eyes met mine, and I felt as if I had huge weights tied to my arms and legs, preventing me from moving. All I could do was look at her. Her blue eyes were deep and dark, as if they held all the secrets of evil. They were as cold as the Arctic, and I was held helplessly in their stare.   Laughing, she declared, "You know who I am. I am Sarah Bishop. And I know who you are. You are Virginia Smith, my husband's lover. Don't you remember?"

At that moment, I remembered everything. I was at the masquerade ball dancing with John Bishop. I was his lover. I was Virginia Smith—or, at least, I was once. Sarah had not killed John because she couldn't have children. She had killed him because he had taken a lover, one who was kind, one who actually loved him.

I was a servant in the house, and I had heard the argument in the cellar and followed John and Sarah into the yard. I had stood in the rain and watched helplessly as John was beheaded. I was the servant who went into town to get help. I was the only one who knew the motive behind the murder of John Bishop. I had never told anyone.

I stood frozen in the rain, having just watched Sarah Bishop behead my lover once again. I wondered how many times she had conducted this unspeakable act throughout the years. How many times had poor John Bishop succumbed to the witch's murderous hands? Just then, to my relief, the gaze of Sarah Bishop was broken by a massive flash of lightning. When it subsided, Sarah and John Bishop were both gone. But blood was all over the yard, even on me.

Suddenly my limbs felt like helium-filled balloons. I bolted across the lawn toward my car. When I reached my car, the storm suddenly subsided. It completely stopped—no lightning, no thunder, no wind and no rain. I was so frightened that I jumped in my car and tried to start it, even though I knew it was dead. Much to my amazement, it started. As I turned the ignition switch, I noticed that my hands and clothes were completely clean, no blood anywhere.

I put the car in gear and, as I drove away, I wondered why Sarah Bishop had chosen that night to lure me into the house, to force regressed memories from a past life to come forward. Then lightning flashed one last time and I saw John Bishop in the yard again. And then I remembered. It was the anniversary of the murder. I swore to myself that I would never pass that house again. And I never have. But the memories of who I once was, what I had witnessed, and the night in the Bishop house still haunt me.

"After attending a dinner party Victoria finds herself on a road she usually avoids because of the Bishop House, a place she's always feared.

Things become worse when unforeseen circumstances cause her to enter the house, wherein, she discovers its terrible secrets and discovers the reason behind her fears.

A thoroughly enjoyable short story."

-Author Susan Keefe-

"I enjoyed this short story, it was very reminiscent of Edgar Allen Poe. Ronda Caudill continues to create interesting characters and story lines. I look forward to more works from this writer."

-Author MD Martin-